A World Split Open

*What would happen if one woman
told the truth about her life?
The world would split open.*

Muriel Rukeyser

A World Split Open

Poems and Prose by
Mildred Farkash Miller

Powderhorn Writers Festival   Minneapolis   1998

Printed in the United States of America by McNaughton & Gunn
Edited by Sue Ann Martinson
Book and cover design by Shari Albers

Published in 1998 by the Powderhorn Writers Festival, a program of
Powderhorn Park Neighborhood Association (PPNA)
3222 Bloomington Avenue South
Minneapolis, Minnesota 55407
612/722-4817 *telephone*
612/721-5799 *fax*
pwf@ppna.org *e-mail*
Books may be ordered from PPNA at the address above.

ISBN 0-9668450-0-5

Thanks are due to the following perodicals and books in which some of these
poems and essays first appeared:
*The Horn, Identity, Northern Sun News, Southwest Journal, The Powderhorn Paper,
Midtown News, Minnesota Women's Press, Minnesota Senior News, Northfield
Magazine, Minnesota Literature, "Fierce with Reality"* edited by
Margaret Cruikshenk, *Close to the Ground: Powderhorn Writers Anthology.*

Cover photos: (front left) Mildred Farkash Miller at five years
            (front right, back) Mildred Farkash Miller today

Third Printing, January 2003
Library of Congress Catalog Card Number: 98-89257
Library of Congress Cataloging-in-Publication Data

Miller, Mildred Farkash, 1920-
        A world split open / Mildred Farkash Miller

ISBN 0-9668450-0-5

Acknowledgements

I wish to thank Shari Albers, Dorothy Sauber,
Nikki LaSorella, Patty Wheeler Andrews,
Victoria Holbert, Betty Sisson, Iola Smith,
Rhoda Lewin, Darson LaPan, Mary Dobish,
Joel Friedman, June Harmon and all my family
and friends for their encouragement.

I also wish to thank Roy McBride,
Jeannie Piekos, Sue Ann Martinson, Warren Park
and Amy Ballestad of the Powderhorn Writers
Festival and Akhmiri Sekhr-Ra and the Arts and
Culture Committee of the Powderhorn Park
Neighborhood Association for their help and
support in publishing this book.

A World Split Open

We are not the things we own

Show me the man who can control a cloud

Holding back the land

For Dorothy Sauber

Who gave me the courage to find my voice

Writing gives me a sense of power

As a woman, an old woman, I am a part of one of the least powerful groups in our society. We are generally portrayed by the media as silly, sentimental, or stupid. Take your pick. Sometimes, all three.

Often treated as invisible, we are not consulted even on matters that concern us, not listened to. Our opinions are not sought; we are discounted, not worthy of time or attention. Our experiences are belittled, we are often the subject of ridicule or demeaning laughter.

Power is what counts. I have found power in writing.

Writing does not come easily to me. It is a difficult task of unearthing layers and layers of years, years spent working simply to earn money to pay our bills and raise our family. Those were full-time jobs that left no time or energy for writing. My only writing was in letters to family and friends, and those letters have long since vanished.

I thought I would remember everything that happened to me. I don't. Distant memory takes on a dream-like quality. I am not certain about some things I seem to remember, and there is no one around to verify them.

Memory plays tricks on us. Sometimes we may have thought for such a long time about taking a trip to a particular place that we aren't sure we've really been there. When I was younger, I had definite ideas about "reality." Now reality is nebulous; it is not so simple. How much was anticipation, what did happen, how does it seem from hindsight? Memory has become three dimensional.

I have learned to bring back tangible evidence (for myself) to prove I've been in a particular place. Sometimes it is only a small white stone washed satin smooth by a constant sea. When I touch it, I know the place I found it, how the sky looked at that moment, the smell of salt in the air, the sea gulls hovering, all the sensations of my senses. The stone is my photograph, my moment captured in time, my token of reality.

I wish I had kept journals during those busy "lost" years my children were growing up. Yes, there are some photos stacked away in a desk drawer, pictures that we sometimes take out, and look at, and laugh at and try to identify. (I didn't always date them.) There are remnants of graduations and special days, but what happened in our daily lives? How did they change so gradually that we were unaware of the changes taking place most of the time? A few words in a journal could have given me a clue now, as I look back and try to see a pattern in my life.

It is only when one is older that one can look back. When we are young, our lives are unfolding. We are making choices, taking one road or another. Sometimes they are deliberate choices; often they are accidental, by chance or circumstance alone. Time has a way of obscuring the reasons for those choices.

Keeping a journal the last few years has taught me the value of being aware of the fragility of time. We squander it, as if it were endless and had no meaning. Writing gives it substance; it becomes almost tangible. In recalling the events and thoughts of an ordinary day, it becomes extraordinary. Sometimes it is only a phrase a friend says in the midst of casual conversation, a joke one hears or noting the red streak of a cardinal across a winter sky.

Often there is an unexpected jog from the rich storehouse of memory of a part of an experience we have not thought about for a long time – a smell or a taste of something, perhaps from childhood, covered up by many, many layers of consciousness.

Writing as a woman of my generation, I have sometimes found I am speaking for my silent sisters, women who have walked in the shadows of men for so long that they do not know what to say or how to say it. They have lost their voices. When I have read to them of our common experiences, they nod their heads in recognition and understanding. When one can speak for oneself, and for others, there is a sense of power. Writing gives me that.

Bones of thought

Seeds

All through the very busy years

Of washing diapers and dishes

Dishes and diapers,

Knee deep in children,

Patching blue jeans,

And making peanut butter sandwiches,

And going to PTA and Scout meetings,

Little league ball games, cheering until hoarse,

My poems stayed inside me

Tiny seeds, silently waiting to be

Set free

Poetry is a web of words

Poetry

Is a web of words

A tiny seductive spider spins

An intricate, sticky web

Trapping tiny drops of truth

Poetry is a skeleton

Poetry is a skeleton

Bones of thought

The words are flesh

They change, they rot away

Bones remain

Poems are seeds

Poems are seeds

Like wild flowers

Growing along the highway

Brilliant and beautiful

Catching the sun,

As common as sky or

Snow or

Grass

No one sees

Words

Words

Are the tools of my trade

The nails and

The hammer

The smell of wood

And sawdust

And the pounding of my heart

We are each of each other

The bookcase my father built

When I think of books and my love of reading, I think of the bookcase my father built.

He was born in a village in Hungary that later became Czechoslovakia. He had little formal education. At twelve he was sent to live as an apprentice with a carpenter in another village. He missed his family, but that was where he learned his trade.

As he approached the age for compulsory military service he decided to go to America. On his sixteenth birthday he arrived, alone, at Ellis Island with the clothes on his back and his skill in his hands.

It was 1907 – hard times. His first two years in this country he lived on bread and grapes, the cheapest food he could buy. He always worked very hard to provide for us and was respected for his honesty and integrity, as well as his exacting craftsmanship.

We didn't have money but, because we never went hungry, we didn't think of ourselves as poor.

Books were our most prized possessions.

My two sisters, brother, and I kept asking him to build us a bookcase. Like the shoemaker's children who needed shoes, we were the carpenter's children who needed a bookcase. One day he surprised us; it was beautiful, and we were very proud.

We had the complete works of Shakespeare and studied two plays a year in high school, memorizing famous passages I still remember. We had Charles Dickens – *David Copperfield, A Tale of Two Cities, A Christmas Carol*, all his works. We had Tolstoy's *Anna Karenina*, and Dostoevski's *Crime and Punishment*. I was surprised when I went to college that many of my classmates hadn't read these books.

We also had *The Gadfly* about an anonymous crusading editor fighting for social justice. It made a deep impression on me.

And in those days of no sexual education there was a book that puzzled me, *The Unmarried Father*. My older sisters told me I was too young for it. I read it secretly.

Books were the key to escape from the limitations of being immigrant working class. We were expected to work hard in school, to be on the honor roll – and we were.

In two generations all my father's grandchildren, all twelve of them, were college graduates. Two of them have doctorates and are college professors.

Humble beginnings, a handmade bookcase, a love of learning.

A rich heritage.

Warm clothes

Couldn't sleep
An address kept running through my head
Of a place I've never seen

Volovitza
Posta Kivyasda
Zupa Bereg
Czechoslovakia

I still hear the love in her voice
As she said, "Print the address big and clear"
And "Spell it like it sounds."
I printed it many times, growing up,
Printed for my mother, to send to her family
Packages of warm clothes, scarfs and gloves,
Jackets, sweaters, even underwear.
Sizes and the colors didn't matter.
We gathered warm clothes each year
Checked to see all the buttons were securely sewed on,
That nothing was torn,
Then wrapped them carefully in heavy brown paper
Tied in double knots with strong cord.
We took them to the post office, watched them
Weighed and measured, paid the price.

Then we waited
To learn they had been received.

We sent clothes for aunts and uncles,
Cousins I had never seen, for my grandparents,
My mother's family whom she would never see again
After she left home alone, at age 13.

Sometimes I wondered why they sent nothing
Back, and mother would say,
"Winters are long and cold in that village
People are poor
They have no money for warm clothes.
They use everything we send, each piece will fit
Someone."
No remnants now, no scraps of cloth,
No fibers left,
Of her name, or
Her father's name, no survivors.
Their land was taken from them, their homes
Destroyed, and they themselves
Disappeared, anonymous match sticks,
Twisted rag dolls, in the ovens of
Auschwitz, Treblinka.

Roots

My friends visit Norway or Scotland
Or Denmark or Ireland
To discover their origins
And ask me
(Because they know I travel)
Whether I have done the same.
I shake my head and do not
Answer.

The fine dust of my kin from the furnaces of
Auschwitz and Treblinka
Has been blown by the fickle wind
All over the world and oceans
And may even be on us now,
Here.

Other aunts, uncles, cousins I never saw
Lie in unmarked mass graves.
I cannot honor them with flowers.
Only with
Remembering.
Wiped out, as if they never existed,
My hundred are part of the
Six million.

No, there is no one left in Europe
I can visit.

Like a horseshoe

Years ago I watched my mother
Work with dough
(No cake mixes then or
Instant anything)

She used her hands and a wooden breadboard
Mixed yeast, milk, flour, butter, sugar and eggs
Not measuring but going by the feel of it
Her hands knowing when to add and when to stop
Working the dough until it was right
Then letting it rise with its own magic

When it was ready she would roll it flat,
Spread butter, cinnamon, raisins, a bit more sugar
Roll it up and let it rise again

Shape it like a horseshoe
Bake it golden brown, then let it cool
Cut a slice for each of us and watch our faces

I can taste it now

The breadboard

My father (your grandpa) was a carpenter, a stair builder,
And cabinet maker, a fine craftsman.
He learned his trade in the old country,
Hungary, before it became Czechoslovakia.
His parents sent him as an apprentice
When he was twelve, to another village.
His eyes spoke of the loneliness of separation.
His father had decided what he should do.
He watched and learned and did
What he was told.

I watched him plane a piece of wood.
It held life and strength and
Became a piece of beauty in his hands.
I liked the smell of sawdust and
The soft thin curls falling down
On the newspaper on the floor.
He had learned to measure, every piece fit exactly.
I wanted him to teach me
But I was a girl, my brother wasn't interested.
We both lost.

A kind and gentle man, he didn't want to be a soldier
(There was compulsory military service)
So he left his home and parents, never to see them again.
He arrived on Ellis Island alone, with the clothes on his back
On his 16th birthday, August 15, 1907.

Work was scarce and hard to find.
He was a hard worker, an honest man who
Never asked for help from anyone, a proud man, always.
He saw the need for unions and worker's rights for
Fair pay, and decent working conditions for all people.

He became a citizen and voted for Eugene Debs, the Socialist,
Twice, and even though Debs lost,
My father always kept his principles.

I was his third (and last) daughter.
I'm sure he wanted a son when I was born.
He called me his "shayna maydela"
I was his favorite.

I wish I remembered a lot more
But my father was a silent, quiet man.
I didn't ask all the questions I
Would ask now.

Once when he visited us
You watched him fix some broken sash cords for a window,
You learned by watching him.

When he and my mother married in 1911
He made her a sturdy oak breadboard
And rolling pin, for pies and cakes,

Homemade noodles, and golden glistening "challah"
For Friday nights.
You watched Grandma roll out leaves of dough
For fine thin egg noodles, you watched her bake "kipelech"
As only she could make them, buttery crescents of
Yeast dough filled with cinnamon, nuts and raisins
That would melt in your mouth

That breadboard is for you now, Steve.

The Mitzvah (good deed)
for Sam

Every year of his long life
That he could remember
The old man had gone to the
Synagogue for morning and evening prayers and
On Shabbat, and all the
Holy Days, always, always on
Rosh Hashanah and Yom Kippur

This year was different
This year he could not go
He was too weak and sick

His learned friend knew how he felt,
Borrowed the Shofar, and brought it
To his apartment, and
After chanting the familiar words, blew
It for him, alone

He had never heard of anyone
To be so honored

The two old men said
Their ancient prayers, held each other,
And wept

Looking at my bird feeder

When the hungry sparrows flock around my
Bird feeder these winter days
I think of Tante Minnie
On Rochambeau Avenue in the Bronx
And how she fed the birds that came
To her fire escape.

She was a kind and gentle woman, an immigrant
From Hungary, an accomplished hatmaker
And dressmaker for wealthy women
Who paid for handmade embroidered silk
Dresses for their children.

She lived in the same tiny apartment
For over fifty years, rarely went out.
Uncle Dave bought groceries – milk and eggs,
And cottage cheese, and a challah and chicken
For Friday night.

They came to our house for Seders.
She fixed the bitter herbs,
She made the charosets – chopped apple
And walnuts with cinnamon and a few drops
Of sour wine. We ate it at the proper time.

I never knew much about her (or Uncle Dave)
Until one day I took a civil service test

At a school in the Bronx, so I went to see
Her. We drank tea and she showed me faded
Photographs of when she and Uncle Dave were
"Keeping Company." They were married in my
Parents' apartment.

She told me World War I came and she was pregnant
And afraid of being left alone while Dave
Went to war. She had an abortion and
Almost died. It left her sterile,
There would be no children.

The war ended before he had to leave
And she had done this needless thing
And there would be no children.

I began to understand
Why she fed the birds
And looked at them
The way she did.

We drank tea together long ago.
She knew how to fix
The bitter herbs.

Almost the end of October

It is almost the end of October
A few leaves are left on some of the trees
Our oak has them all, and
Fiery scarlet they are, more beautiful than ever.
The great grandmother sits on the
Red swing, she wears many layers of clothes,
And is wrapped in three woolen blankets.

She tilts her head to catch the angle of
The waning sun, feeling its warmth
On her weathered, wrinkled cheeks.
She watches the black and white
Junco snatch the sunflower seeds
From the bird feeder, one at a time,
Hungry, coming back each time for
One more.

A black cat with copper colored eyes
Slinks through the vegetable garden
Which is finished for the year. But the red rose bush
Still has three roses on it, one
Of them is a bud, tightly folded into itself.

The sun is going down
The air is colder now
It is time to go in

My mother

She is there
At the window
Watching, and waiting for us
When we come, and waves.

We bring groceries and news
Of each other

We eat soup and toasted bread
And they have a special taste
Only there.

We look at old photographs and
Talk and laugh together.

She loses that lost, lonely look
She had when we came.
Her face is alive again.

We plan our next visit
And when we drive away
She is there again
At the window
One hand supporting the other
So she can wave to us
Again
As we go.

After one week in a nursing home

The paint is peeling from your finger nails
Your hair is getting long and straggly
You need a haircut

The nurses aides dress you up like a mannequin
Prop you up in a wheelchair
Put lipstick on your lips
And even the glasses you never wanted to wear
Are slipping down on your nose
As I wheel you into the dining room
For your baby food supper

One word, mother, say just one word,
Any word
And

You and I will plot your escape from
These rooms where death cowers in
Corners, behind curtains,
Everywhere

The smell of death
And bent bodies and broken minds
Shattered like slivers of glass
In the smooth impersonal hallways

You have chosen silence now

Resolute and proud
With a strong sense of justice
You always stood
As tall as you could
And spoke your mind

Now that you are a husk,
A shell of your former self
You do not scream or babble
No whimpering here, no cry for pity,
No tears

You could find the words

But with great dignity and strength
You have chosen silence

To contain
Your anger
And your pain

Beyond further need for language

When I see you in that room
Shrunk in to yourself
Your eyes shutting out your world
The TV blasting away, no one
Looking at it or listening to it,
The others slumped in their wheelchairs
Or strapped in so they won't fall out
I put my face close to yours
So you can see
Familiar territory, oh remember
Please remember me

"Hello, hi, Mom
How are you?"

You open your eyes and I wait, I wait
For that spark to light the fire
To make the connection, to say
My name

It is a gift you can give me, all I
Want, all I ask for now.

Thank you, thank you.

All our conversations every day
On the phone are history, memory
For me. (I don't know what they are for you)

I tell you about everyone in the family
All the names and news of them

You smile and watch my lips
I don't know what you hear
Or what it means to you
(It's not for me to judge)

You hold my hand very tightly
Silently keep looking at my face
Until it's time to go. I say
"We all love you" as I kiss you goodbye.

Then, as if on rusty hinges
From deep within the well of you
Sounding very, very far away
I hear you say,
"I love you, too."

Dying by centimeters

You are almost always sleeping now
When I see you
Dreaming your own private dreams
No one can enter

You have left us behind
The way a snake slowly sheds its skin
Or a creature of the sea
Leaves its shell upon the sand

With nothing left to consume
You are consuming yourself

Etched in stone upon my brain

You leave behind
Fossils
Of memory

Last freedom

What do you dream of
Little mother
In your narrow cell
Old age crib
Raised up bars of steel
How your world has
Shrunk

Suitcases in my basement
Bulging with what you leave behind
Only your dreams
Fly like unleashed kites
In the wild winter wind

I didn't ask this question and now it's too late

Mother

Do you remember the day

I was five years old and we

Had just moved to New Jersey to the

Only house we ever owned

(We lost it during the Depression)

I was playing with my brother

He was three and couldn't do much

But we wanted to play with these new kids

Until they started throwing stones at us

And called us dirty Jews

And Christ-killers

Who was Christ, I wondered

I was just a little girl, I never killed anything

And I ran to you into the house, crying

And told you what was going on

You took my hand

And my brother's

And with a look on your face

I have never forgotten

You walked with us

To the police station
And told the policemen,
"We are new here,
My children have the right to be here,
This is America,
Not Europe,
We are not hurting anyone"

One of the policemen
Walked back with us
And told the children to stop
Throwing stones

You taught me how to be
A woman

To my sister

March 30
Dear Ruth

Your package came today
(I wasn't expecting anything)

When you called last week
And told me you were cutting pussy willows
In your garden
You must have sensed the hunger
I felt here in Minnesota where
The calendar says spring
But the wind has a wintery howl

Inside the box were
Pussy willows, soft fuzzy catkins
Had fallen off the branches
There in a plastic bag, all in a heap
Like many years ago
When I was working in Washington, D.C.
Christmas time and I was alone
You sent me a box of cookies
I couldn't tell their shape, they were
All crumbs.
I ate them with a spoon

Pussy willows, and cookie crumbs

Marriage is not a tug of war

The silken bonds that tie us
Slip and slide
As sometimes you
Or sometimes I
Must change and grow
And give up something
That we did before
We said we would be
One

I'll give you time
And space
To be yourself
If you will do the same
For me

We'll trust each other
And come back each time stronger
In our love, than we were
Before
Marriage is not a tug of war

Our first house

We lived
In that four room house
For fifteen years
How did we ever do it.
All six of us.

In summer we had a garden
In the back yard
Remember the first year
How lushly everything grew
The big red tomatoes and green beans
And long cucumbers
We were astonished
Then we remembered
The couple who had lived there before
Had done a lot of fishing
And buried the bones of the dead fish
In the ground
We made into a garden.

Remember the picnics on the front lawn
Of peanut butter sandwiches
We were shaded by the catalpa tree
Whose white blossoms
Perfumed our bedroom window upstairs

And then dropped long brown seedpods
Our children played with.

In winter I wanted
To push out the walls,
(You called it snug)
I wanted closets
And a space to call my own,
(You liked the closeness)
But I was knee deep
In children, all day long.

You built a sandbox for them
And later turned the back yard into a
Skating rink; they pushed the wooden
Kitchen chairs around, and held on,
And learned to skate that way.

When it rained one night you went out
And brought in the soaking limp rag doll
Someone was crying for.

There was a gate,
I was always closing it.

The rain pours down in a steady stream

The rain pours down in a steady stream
Thunder and lightning interrupt
My sleep
It's not yet five and I am wide awake
I get up to check the windows once again
I know they are closed, but I still check
I look at the empty beds
That once held children.
Father and mother we were
Needed and necessary, ready to comfort
And reassure, to listen to bad dreams
And listening, dissolve them.

Who will listen now to my dreams
In this empty house
As the rain pours down

Your father is not dead

Your father is not dead

How can he be

When I am part of him

And he was part of me?

And you, you are of us both.

We are each

Of each other

Who is to say

Where one begins

And the other ends?

One day

One day

I will join you

In the deep, dark earth

And our bones will mingle

As our flesh once did

And we will be

One

Again.

Another way?

One of my sons says

"Why do you answer

Every question

With another question?"

And I say

"Is there another way?"

Only the young

Only the young

Have answers

For all the questions

Benjamin at four

Knew it all.

"No grandma, don't tell me.

I know."

Where does all that knowledge go?

We are not the things we own

Old older oldest

We're all lumped together
Like cold mashed potatoes,
Leftovers.
Sixty or over ninety, it doesn't matter,
If your hair turns grey
And you don't dye it
Another color,
Or wear a wig, like some of my friends—
You are thought of as
Old and sexless.
And then you are invisible.
No lust or longing in men's eyes
No recognition that you still have much to
Offer – to give, and receive.

Walk down the street and no one
Looks you in the eye, except maybe
Another
"Old" woman, who smiles knowingly.

Your body, once your friend,
Is now
Your enemy.

The only other ones who notice
Are children on the bus,
Strangers, who call you
Grandma.
Their young mothers smile, without understanding.

The quality of life

Getting older
Is like
Trying to keep afloat
In a leaky boat

Plug up one hole
And you spring a leak
Somewhere else

All you determined joggers and
Fitness freaks

Do you think about
The quality of life
Your extra years
Will bring?

Living longer
Is not enough

Pepsi generation
Just you wait

The sign on the house

The Red River flood had claimed it all

The house they had lived in

And everything in it they had worked for

Piled in front waiting to be taken away

But what I remember most

Was the sign on the house

Which read:

We are not the things we own

New age

You called me. I wasn't home

You left a message

I called back, you weren't there

It's great to get and give messages

But when our machines talk to each other

Will we still remember how?

Even that

We were talking about Virginia Woolf

Her books, her thoughts, and how she died

Walking into deep dark water with

Stones in her pockets

When one woman told about her daughter

Who had tried to cut her wrists

And the girl's father, a doctor, told her

"You didn't do it right, even that

You didn't do right"

The mother said it was funny, and yet

It wasn't funny.

No one laughed. No one

Scraps of time

I am terminal
But still greedy for life

I have no time to waste
Give me the minutes you spend
Fussing and fuming, impatiently
Waiting in rush hour traffic or
The check out line at Target,
Kmart or Holiday Plus

I'll take parts of minutes, seconds,
Scraps of time, crumbs, leftovers
They'll add up, those
Infinitesimal hungry moments

My rag bag of chaos
Will become my unique pattern

My life and legacy
My woman quilt

Carpe diem

Busy all the time, both of us

With four small kids

My neighbor and I

Washing clothes and dishes,

Cleaning, patching blue jeans

She asked me to come in

For a cup of coffee

"Too busy" I said

The next day she was killed

Driving Girl Scouts home from camp

No audience

Getting old is like

Being in a play

Rehearsing all your lines

Until you have it down pat –

Gestures, nuances,

Every detail.

And then no one comes

There's no audience

Everyone's busy,

Somewhere else

So long ago

We walked through the old monastery together

You, almost blind, felt comfortable in the dim light

Of the cavernous silence

While I described the bright colors of the stained glass

Windows

Testing my memory of saints and sinners

We whispered, even in the garden

Where there was no need for whispers

Why do I remember this, of so long ago?

Passion

There is no love

But of this moment's loving

This purging

Of all pent-up emotion

That feels nothing

Having felt all.

Even now

As I scrub the kitchen floor

And vacuum the worn out

Rug in the living room,

As I wash the dishes

And make my bed,

My embryonic poems stretch and

Grow, and change, and

Kick

A different adjective

(A tiny toe nail?)

A stronger verb

(A strand of hair?)

Even now,

The mother

Friends

Are as necessary as sun

And rain, and the air we breathe.

They help us become ourselves

And accept us as we are.

They laugh with us, tell funny stories

And cry with us

When we are hurt.

They help us stretch our minds

And grow,

They enrich our lives

There is no one here but me

There is no one here but me
No one to talk to

Or listen to

No one who will get an aspirin for me
When I have a headache
Or cannot sleep
Or say "God bless you"
When I sneeze.

No one to help with decisions,
To warm my cold feet
Or aching heart.

There's no one to argue with
To blame for things I haven't done
To laugh with
Or cry with or
Even be bored or angry with.

There's no one here but me
And the air and the empty rooms
And the ticking of the clock
The beating of my heart
And the rest is
Silence.

A modern fable

Once upon a time
There was a beautiful park
Called Powderhorn, from its shape of long ago,
Forgotten now.
There were many trees, all sizes and shapes
Green in spring, orange and scarlet and brown
In autumn, soft white in winter.
One year, many trees were cut down
Bugs had eaten them away, some were lightning-struck.
The people who loved the park
Complained, and asked for trees to replace the lost ones.
But the Park Board said,
"You have enough. No one notices those that are gone."
Each year, after that
More trees died, for one reason or another,
Like people, they were simply gone and not replaced.
It was all open space now, no trees to stop the sky,
Until someone said,
"Weren't there trees here once upon a time
In this park?"
And the children asked,
"What's a tree?"

To my children and my friends

To my children and my friends

And anyone who may have loved me

No tears, please

When I die

No pity.

For I

Have had a good life

A full life

A rich life

All that I have ever wanted.

Remember me kindly,

If you can,

Be good to one another

And

Be happy.

I am a thorn

I am a thorn

A thorn that protects a rose

And if you come

Too close

I will prick you and

Make you bleed.

You will know

You have been near

Me.

Listen:

Love is here

All around.

As constant

As the air that moves

In and out, amidst these hollow chimes.

Unseen, untouchable, everlasting

Stronger than death.

To the sweet music of life,

Listen!

Reach out, reach out

Reach out

Reach out

And try to touch the

Mind of someone else

With a look,

A smile,

A word,

A touch,

Or we are all lost.

Escape, escape

Escape, escape
There's no escape

Some go to a priest
Others to a shrink
Some pop pills
For imaginary ills
While others
Merely drink.

Some can whore
Forever more
And never question why.

For the pain, my sweet
Is very, very deep

So, if you wonder why
I'll just go on
And write my poems
And then, perhaps
I'll sleep.

Show me the man
who can control a cloud

The day I became a feminist

I remember it very clearly.

I was a freshman at a Teachers College in New Jersey, and one of the required classes was "World Outlook." It was 1938.

One of the class projects was to choose a topic and give a written and oral report on it. We had a long list to choose from. I chose "The Role of Women in our Society." No one else picked it.

I went to the college library looking for material. Nothing.

Undaunted, I decided to go to the New York Public Library, one of the biggest and best in this country. I took a bus, ferry, subway and another bus. I asked for books or articles on the role of women. Nothing. I couldn't find anything.

I made several trips, thinking all the time it was my fault. I was up against a wall of silence. I was very frustrated, but remember, this was 1938, more than fifty years ago.

Without outside sources I had to write my paper from my own thoughts and observations, so I wrote about the choices women had. Those were Depression years, and few women went to college. I was one of the lucky ones.

Women could be teachers, or nurses, or secretaries or sales clerks. Or they could get married and have children. Men were the breadwinners, very few women worked outside the home. In many places women teachers who married were forced to resign. Men could keep their jobs. Restrictions were the rule rather than the exception.

I wrote that women ought to be free to be whatever they wanted to be – doctors, lawyers, engineers, artists, etc. and use all their talent. That talent and those gifts deserved to be recognized, rewarded and appreciated. Women ought to be able to support themselves. Getting married or not should be an individual choice, not based on societal pressure or economic necessity. Women should be free to make their own choices about their careers, marriage and how they wanted to live.

Radical ideas. Fortunately, my professor was a liberal thinker. He listened, so did the class.

I got an "A" for my report and the course.

I didn't know it then, but by questioning the status quo, I had become a feminist.

No nukes

We could use energy
From the sun,
Water,
Wind,
The earth itself

Natural elements
That we understand

Instead
Men, in their arrogance,
Defy nature
And create energy
They cannot control,
Creating waste they
Cannot dispose,
Leaving us all vulnerable
No matter where we live
On this fragile earth
To the deadly winds of
Radioactivity

Show me the man
Who can control a
Cloud

Mister President

If nuclear bombs are dropped
They will kill poets and rapists alike
Presidents and priests
Doctors and children and ministers
And bank robbers and murderers.

The workers who built the bombs
(it gave them jobs)
Will be as dead as the dogs and cats and rats
In the street.
The remains and rubble
Will be left to the insects and rats.

Who will inherit the earth,
Mister President?

Questions

Elie Wiesel won
The Nobel Prize for Peace

He lived, just barely, through
Auschwitz, Birkenau, Bina, and Buchenwald.

He saw a truckload of babies
Dumped into a fire.
He watched while his dying father's head
Was smashed by a guard.

He survived against all the laws of chance,
All the laws of probability.

He was silent for ten years
Then he began to write
With a soul on fire.

How many potential Nobel Prize winners
Lie murdered in the broken bones of the
Six million?

And in the wars since,
And going on this minute

(Read your daily newspaper)
World leaders play word ga
On what is offense and
What is defense
While nuclear weapons
Lie incubating
Like giant deadly rotten eggs
Waiting for the press of a button.

The people sleep, apathetic,
Pursuing only their self-interest.
They allowed one Holocaust to happen.
Will they wake in time, before the last,
To be human to one another?

Why

Why

In this land of record harvest

And plowed under fields

Are there

Hungry children

And homeless in church basements

Food shelves

Always waiting to be filled

Bag ladies and

Street people in one of the

Richest countries in the

World

Tiananmen Square

In Beijing
In Tiananmen Square
One incredible man, silently
Stood alone, unarmed,
Defiantly facing a line of armored tanks.

Moving a few steps to his right
The first tank moved to the right.

He moved to his left
The tank moved to the left.

This deadly stalking lion and mouse game went on
Until his friends came,
Hustling him off to safety.

He knew one tank can crush a man
Hundreds, even thousands of men

But guns and tanks cannot crush an idea
The hungry need for freedom
The crying need for freedom
The old, new need for freedom

As long as one brave human being
Lives.

Surplus commodities

Mister President*
You are a senior citizen

Why don't you stand in line
With these seniors, silently waiting
With their empty shopping bags
And cardboard boxes
For a box of powdered milk,
"American" cheese,
And sometimes
Butter, stored so long it has no taste,
(Where is the expiration date?)
And sometimes, a special treat, like
A bag of rice, or
Flour

Then you could wait on the corner

For a bus to take you home
Like the rest of us

* *Ronald Reagan*

Explaining the U.S.A.

This is the land of opportunity –

You have the right to be poor,
You have the right to be unemployed,
You have the right to be hungry and homeless.

You have the right to be illiterate
Even after graduating from high school,
If you can read
You have the right to read magazines
That show women put into meat grinders.

You have the right to put a white hood
Over your face
And burn your neighbor's house
Because you don't like her religion
Or the color of his skin.

You have the right to die because you
Don't have medical insurance.

You have the right to drink acid rain,
And watch trains carrying nuclear waste
That will last
For who knows for how long.

You have all these rights and more

Because you are free

In this land of opportunity

Clean hands

When you talk of freedom, my friend
Talk about corporations
That close their factories
Leaving their faithful workers
With no pensions or prospects
And move to another state,
Or another country
Alabama, Mexico, Korea,
It's a small world.
(Companies need no passports or visas
Or permission, of any kind)

There is always a place
Where wages are lower,
So they can reap
Larger profits

And who are the workers
Who sit at sewing machines,
Or stand or sit at assembly lines
For long hours, for little pay,
In every country, including ours

They are women
For the most part
Women who work
To feed hungry children

Men with telephones sit at computers
In the front office
Men with white shirts and clean hands
Busy, figuring out
Their next move
For still larger profits

They father the children
Women feed them

Tell me about freedom

Words

Many words or few
It is all the same

Man should have been as silent
As the beasts, the stones, the trees

For words confuse and alter
They build walls that should not be

They kill, they maim, they slaughter

It is all the same
Many words or few

In memoriam

Women in Nicaragua
In Ireland
In Afghanistan
In this country
And every country
You can name
Give up their men
To their leaders
Who call them "boys"
And sometimes blow bugles
When they die

Take back your medals
They are empty symbols
Of a lost faith in
Justice

Take back your folded flag
Precisely cornered
Neatly folded

It does not take the place
Of the man you called a boy
And sent to die

363 days

Food baskets
For the poor
At Thanksgiving and
Christmas
Fill their bellies
For a few days.

Who cares about
the other
363 days of the
Year?

Lest we forget

I swam in the pool in Munich
The Olympic pool of 1972.
Later, in my dreams,
I saw the pool again
But this time it was not filled
With water.
The water had turned to blood
And blood was running over
The sides of it, it was so full
As before
And the digital clock on the wall
That changed each minute
Was counting instead the slaughtered Jews.

Germany is rich again,
Strong again,
And the blood spills over the
Sides of the pool.

Evening news

I watch the evening news on TV

A mother in Ethiopia forces an infant
To swallow a little milk

The old, misshapen face spits it back
Starving too long, it has forgotten
How to eat.

Commercials follow
Selling

Buicks

Microwaves

Croissants

The baby dies

Equal appetite

The white garbage truck comes up
Our alley every Monday morning about 6 a.m.

Sometimes I go out with my last
Contribution, just before it comes.

Yesterday I saw a mattress in the alley
(Clean, in good shape, nothing wrong with it that I could see)
With a note taped to it, "Salvation Army"
The wind blew the note off, twice I put it back.
But it must have blown away again
Because the next time I looked
The hungry jaws of the garbage truck were
Chewing up the mattress.

It could have been a haven for lovers,
Or a birthing, or safe place to die.

Last week I read about a homeless man who climbed into a dumpster.
Sunday night, he didn't know the schedule of the white army
Dark and warm inside, he fell asleep.
It was the wrong place to be.
Next morning the operator of the garbage truck didn't stop
In time.

Our efficient garbage trucks eat men and mattresses
With equal appetite.

Human rights

When one woman is degraded
All women are diminished.

When one man goes to war
And kills or hurts another man,
Or child or woman,
All mankind shrivels and shrinks.

When one child is abused
All children are less than they can be.

Each of us is part of the whole
Each has the right to be
Whole.

Holding back the land

The pleasures of aging

The pleasures of aging. You must be kidding. We live in a culture that glorifies youth, strength, motion. Those images are flaunted before us constantly. Only a young, naive whippersnapper would consider anything else. Someone who repeats the old cliche about getting older and "it's better than the alternative."

But there are pleasures of aging. In my seventies I am qualified, by that fact alone, to speak.

For me the greatest pleasure of aging is the freedom I finally have. All the roles I've filled as daughter, student, teacher, wife, mother, concerned citizen, writer, etc., are part of my present and past. I can cultivate the ones I choose to remember and ignore the others. I can, at last, be myself and define that identity in my own terms. In my younger years I could not do that. Each role meant new commitments, new responsibilities, new demands on my time and energy.

I can let go of all the "shoulds." "Today I am expected to do this. I should do that." Now I can set my own agenda, my own priorities.

I can simplify my life. I can ignore pressure and say I do not need that or I have enough. I can give things away. There is power in refusal.

I am not as afraid of failure as I once was. One learns to live with rejection, not take it personally, accept it, and move on.

I took a watercolor painting class in my 60s. After looking at paintings in museums all my life I finally tried to see what I could do. I was amazed that I could do anything. The same is true with writing. We all have tremendous potential we don't use.

And I have a sense of history, of all that has happened in my lifetime to me and the rest of the world. I have survived Depression years, World War II, the Korean War, Vietnam, the wars since and the most recent. I am learning to live with a sense of loss – losing health, family, friends.

In spite of all that, I enjoy living. I am exquisitely aware of how precious and fragile life is; how short, no matter how many years one has. My time is limited. There will never be enough for all the books I want to read, music I want to listen to, people and places I am curious about.

I am still growing and learning and looking forward to new experiences, making new friends, telling old stories.

I am trying to enjoy old age.

After all, I've never been old before.

Illusion

When I first began to travel
I really was naive
To save money on a trip to Hawaii
I agreed to share a room with a stranger

On the plane I noticed a woman
(So did everyone else)
Cute, slim, life of the party
Always laughing, joking
There was no doubt she was having a
Good time

At the hotel in Honolulu she turned out
To be my roommate

When she went to bed
She took off her
Wig
Eye lashes
Finger nails
Teeth
Breasts

I kept wondering what else
She had to shed

She was a small old woman
No one would have noticed

At the "Y"

I swim at the "Y" on Wednesdays
And try to see how many laps I can do
In an hour.
There is a string of flags across the pool
Red, blue, white – red, blue, white –
I count from one end and think now
I am up to this flag, but sometimes
I talk to someone, and then I don't remember
My place in the flags.
I go down the slow lane.
Later I shower with five other women

Some have sagging breasts and bellies
Others are young and firm, slim and tight-skinned.

I think of Rubens and Renoir and Picasso,
How they would have loved to see these
Naked women.
One woman keeps her suit on
While she showers
And I wonder why
Until the day I catch a glimpse
Of her crouching in a corner near the wall,
Undressing. She has only one
Breast.
I pretend I did not see.

The visit

My leg aches as

I pass a neighbor's house

And her husband comes out

On the porch

"How are you?" I say

"How's your wife?"

"Not good," he says.

"Would you like to come in?"

I step into the house

She is on the couch.

I see pillows and blankets and quilts

(It's not a cold day)

And only her face,

A porcelain doll's face

Smooth and pale

Fragile and strong

With bright brown eyes

That strangely, have a sparkle

In them I did not expect.

I look only at her eyes.

She is dying of cancer

I know, and he knows, and

She knows, but we do not

Say the words.

"We are waiting for the nurse," she says.

"She comes three times a week."

"I can't hold her anymore.

I'm afraid I'll drop her"

The husband says, his voice breaking.

"It's in her bones"

"It could be worse," she says, with

A wry smile.

And I wonder

How, how, could it be worse?

I leave the house,

My leg doesn't ache

Anymore.

Two women

Edna, bent over but not broken
Gave me a jar of her wild grape jelly today.
It was wrapped in several layers of paper towels
Held with rubber bands.
She gave it to me quietly and secretly
So the others didn't see.
She often brings roses or Oriental poppies
From her garden, or cookies she has baked.
She is always sharing herself with the rest of us.
I hope I will be making jelly and giving it to friends
When I am 93.

Bea, on the other hand, is just as old. She brought a sample
Of her handmade teddy bears. This one was dressed in a knitted
Santa Claus suit. He had a pointed nose just like hers.
It was for sale, she doesn't give anything away.
There weren't any buyers. I wouldn't give it to
Any kid I liked.

She brought a cake once
Cut in small pieces, one piece for each,
No second helpings.

Identity

Once, at the nursing home
When we were visiting my mother,
A woman approached, tall and thin
And smiling hesitantly, as if she
Wanted to be part of our circle of warmth,
And I said, without thinking, "Hello,
What is your name?"

She looked lost and bewildered
Putting her hand in her empty pocket
Of her cotton dress
And coming up empty-handed, said
"I don't know. I once
Had a name."

Later, I heard a nurse call her
Rachel. Now whenever I see her
There, I say, "Hello, Rachel."
She smiles, as I try to give her
Back
Her name

Letting go
for Sam

You'd lost one son, years ago

And now another,

Both young men

In their prime,

Full of promise.

Only one more left.

It was too much to talk about.

I know.

We both carried the heavy stone

Of grief, in our hearts.

And yet, remember the day

We walked in the park

And stopped to watch

Something neither of us had ever seen

A mother duck was leading her brood

In the middle of the lake

All lined up they were, in regular formation,

As ducks usually do

Until one baby duck couldn't keep up with the others.

It was drowning, there in the middle of the lake.

The mother beat her wings frantically as

She circled her brood, round and round

She went, with a shrieking sound.

We watched, as helpless as she.

In a few minutes she stopped,

She knew she couldn't save it.

She went back to the head of the line

Leading the ones who could survive.

We looked at each other

And went on walking

Content to simply be

I swim on my left side

At my own pace, slowly,

To the deep end of the pool

Then kick off, on my back

And pretend I am a canoe,

Or frog, or

Turtle

And quietly, in the gentle

Yielding water, the primordial water

Of the salty, long ago beginnings of

Life, I am in the softly, rocking waters

Of the womb, with no demands upon me,

Content to simply

Be

At the reviewal

The Scandinavians I live among

Have a different way of looking at

Death

They do not tear their clothes

Or weep

Or beat their breasts as they curse

The unfairness of it all

Instead, they stand in little groups,

And smile at each other

And say, "Doesn't she look nice" and

"I suppose it's better this way"

As they sip their lemonade

And eat their jello and hot dishes

Birds

Some single old women

Flock together, like birds,

And live in public "high risers"

Or expensive condominiums

They shield each other

From the world outside

They play cards

Shop

Have lunch

Visit their doctors and

Hairdressers

Then return, before dark

To their empty nests

Women

Women have kept civilizations from disappearing.

Men, with their constant wars keep trying to annihilate life

Changing borders, killing over the possession of land.

If the earth will be saved, it will be by women.

Some women

Are like boulders

Along a rocky shore

Beaten down by wind

Waves and weather

Washing over us, chipping away

We remain

Strong and solid, holding back

The land from washing into

The sea

Autumn

This is the time of year

I drink in all the glorious colors

Of the trees that cathedral arch

Across the streets, meeting and

Touching each other

One last time

For soon it will be winter

And only charcoal skeletal patterns

Will be etched against the blue cold sky

Reminding me then, of other

Possibilities

Winter

Bears have the right idea

Sleeping through the long cold winter

Barely breathing

Saving their energy

For the sweet honey of spring

Minnesota winter

Winter in Minnesota

Is for the young,

They can scamper over

The mounds of ice and snow

At street crossings

Like white mountain goats,

Sure-footed, unafraid,

Young hips mend swiftly

And besides, they do not fall

So they have no reason to fear.

But I walk gingerly

Three blocks to the Co-op

For yogurt and milk

In the once white streets

Now grey and black and

Yellow streaked, where dogs

Have left their mark,

And I come home, at last,

Breathless, from the cold

Adversity builds character

Someone once said.

She must have been a

Minnesotan.

When an old woman

When an old woman

Who had lived through the Depression

Saw the ocean for the first time

She looked at it for a long time

And finally said:

"It's the first time I've seen anything

that there's enough of"

Silence

In this noisy hectic world

Where we are constantly bombarded by sound

When we want to honor someone

We stop

For a moment of silence

Silence

More eloquent than words

In summer

In summer I watch

The progression of flowers

That bloom and fade

And fill my eyes with color

And the air with their lovely scents.

This is a city I live in

Yet almost everyone has room

For grass and trees and flowers.

First the crocuses under the snow,

Then lilacs and tulips and peonies,

Roses and marigolds and cosmos,

And so many others I cannot name.

Lord, let me remember all this beauty of

These vibrant colors, and this teeming life

In the white stillness of a

Frozen January.

My mother's flower garden

I will gather seeds

This day

From the flower garden

You planted last

Mother's Day

When you put so many seeds in

There was no room for weeds.

All summer those who passed this way

Stopped to enjoy your beautiful patch of flowers.

I will fill the old Crisco can

With promises and hope.

End of summer

My wild and wooly garden

Is full of weeds

They have a beauty of their own

Not of order, but of chaos

Natural and uninhibited

Birds come to eat the tiny seeds

Of the weeds, squirrels absentmindedly

Bury what they find and can't remember

Where they put it

I look at the garden and

See the bird in me and

The squirrel in me

And even the beautiful chaotic weeds

Indian summer

There are days in October

Such as this

That are more like spring

Than spring itself,

The trees, bare of leaves,

Except for the tenacious oak,

Seem ready to burst into flower

Instead of having given up all their leaves.

The air is soft and warm

And one rose bush has buds and red roses

That the cold brush of winter

Can nip off, without warning,

At any time.

Part of memory

I picked the last tomatoes
In the garden today
Even the small hard green ones
Although some I threw back
To nourish the soil for next year.

There's frost predicted for tonight.

It was a good summer
With lots of rain (we hardly had to water,
the rain barrel is still full)

There were plenty for us and
To share with friends, and
The squirrels who brought half eaten
Ones and left them on my porch
For me to see.

The wind is cold now, telling me
This is over, part of memory.

I like beginnings more than
Endings

I know an old woman

I know an old woman who lives alone

And for a whole week spoke to no one

Until she went out

For bread and milk

And then, the first words addressed to her

Were, "Paper or plastic?"

I am a woman

I am a woman.

Even the word "woman" has "man" in it.

We have lived in the shadows of men

First, it is our father's

Or our brother's

Later, it is our husband's

Or our son's (and daughters, wishing they

Were men).

We want to be ourselves,

Complete, alone. Not because we want to be

Alone, but because we are

Human. Even the word "human" has "man"

In it.

We need each other, women and men

Let us be friends,

But only as equals.

Less than a woman

She was a great teacher

Loved literature and inspired

Her students with that same love

For the force, the beauty, the power

Of language

They remembered her

She wasn't spared the nightmare

Of breast cancer

Being prepped for a double mastectomy

The last thing she heard

Before the anaesthetic took effect was

"She won't miss them

She's only a nun"

Cancer, again

My days and nights are all mixed up

I can sleep on the couch by day

At night I think and read Bill Holm's

The Dead Get By With Everything

And think tomorrow I will set the date

That efficient surgeon with no bedside manner

Will take my pound of flesh

Carve away and throw away

My left breast, in the garbage can

Will I then be like the woman

In the "Y" locker room, cowering in a corner

Or will I let the other showering naked women

See my altered body and know the unsuspected,

Invisible, insidious enemy within

Radiation treatment

I lie down on the narrow cool steel table

My left arm is strapped away from my body

As I clutch a bar to hold it in place.

The table can move forward and backward

And to its sides

The radiation machine can move many angles

I must lie still

My chest is a map of measurements

Co-ordinates to the second decimal place.

The radiation therapy technicians measure,

Adjust, and measure again

Finally all is set

They leave the room to press a button.

For thirty seconds the invisible rays

Penetrate my being

A computer has spit out the treatment formula

I close my eyes and

Think of other places I have been and

Hope to see

Hospital roommate

I enjoyed the peace and silence

For one whole day and night

Until you came and you were

Instantly bored

Turning on soap operas

Slamming doors,

Thrashing around in bed

Coughing all over our small room

Dragging your IV downstairs

Standing outside in the cold snow

For another cigarette

The last straw came when

You finally fell asleep

And snored

Hello, house

Home from the hospital

Hello, house

As my mother used to say

(No matter where she lived)

When she saw her familiar door

Knowing she was

Home

The will to live

Noises of the night go on

Whether I am here or not

Refrigerator goes off and on

Whether I am here or not

Crickets chirping in late summer

Whether I am here or not

Clocks ticking away every precious hour

Whether I am here or not

I want to be here

Lord, let me be here

A *new beginning*

The trees outside my window

Stand waiting patiently for a

Day or night of gentle, welcome rain

And then a little sunshine

To burst into spreading leaf

No free will here, no choice

Of where to be, or chance to change,

Start over somewhere else

Choices all made by other

Authority

They bend and sway and do not

Break,

Hold fast their appointed space

Through fierce storms and lightning strikes,

Live within their limitations

And teach us one kind of

Survival

August morning

My fingers smell of parsley now

As I scissor the emerald sprigs growing in the

Inverted black tire at the foot of my back

Steps

In January, God willing,

When the icy wind rattles my windows

I will cook soup

With all good things in it

And

Add some of this August morning

Blue sky and soft breeze

Turning my wind chimes, and brushing them gently

One against the other,

Remembering this time

On the red swing